Dear Parents:

Congratulations! Your child is taking the first steps on an exciting journey. The destination? Independent reading!

STEP INTO READING® will help your child get there. The program offers five steps to reading success. Each step includes fun stories and colorful art or photographs. In addition to original fiction and books with favorite characters, there are Step into Reading Non-Fiction Readers, Phonics Readers and Boxed Sets, Sticker Readers, and Comic Readers—a complete literacy program with something to interest every child.

Learning to Read, Step by Step!

Ready to Read   Preschool–Kindergarten
• big type and easy words • rhyme and rhythm • picture clues
For children who know the alphabet and are eager to begin reading.

Reading with Help   Preschool–Grade 1
• basic vocabulary • short sentences • simple stories
For children who recognize familiar words and sound out new words with help.

Reading on Your Own   Grades 1–3
• engaging characters • easy-to-follow plots • popular topics
For children who are ready to read on their own.

Reading Paragraphs   Grades 2–3
• challenging vocabulary • short paragraphs • exciting stories
For newly independent readers who read simple sentences with confidence.

Ready for Chapters   Grades 2–4
• chapters • longer paragraphs • full-color art
For children who want to take the plunge into chapter books but still like colorful pictures.

STEP INTO READING® is designed to give every child a successful reading experience. The grade levels are only guides; children will progress through the steps at their own speed, developing confidence in their reading.

Remember, a lifetime love of reading starts with a single step!

Copyright © 2023 Disney Enterprises, Inc. All rights reserved. Published in the United States by Random House Children's Books, a division of Penguin Random House LLC, 1745 Broadway, New York, NY 10019, and in Canada by Penguin Random House Canada Limited, Toronto, in conjunction with Disney Enterprises, Inc.

Step into Reading, Random House, and the Random House colophon are registered trademarks of Penguin Random House LLC.

Visit us on the Web!
rhcbooks.com

Educators and librarians, for a variety of teaching tools, visit us at RHTeachersLibrarians.com

ISBN 978-0-7364-4403-3 (trade) — ISBN 978-0-7364-9041-2 (lib. bdg.)
ISBN 978-0-7364-4404-0 (ebook)

Printed in the United States of America   10 9 8 7 6 5 4 3 2 1

Random House Children's Books supports the First Amendment and celebrates the right to read.

Disney

WISH

MADE FROM STARS

adapted by Kathy McCullough

illustrated by the Disney Storybook Art Team

Random House 🏠 New York

Asha lives with her mother, Sakina,
and her grandfather Sabino.
In the kingdom of Rosas,
each person can give their wish
to powerful King Magnifico.
Every month, he grants one wish.

Today is Sabino's birthday!

Asha hopes the king

will finally grant Sabino's wish.

With her pet goat, Valentino,

Asha says goodbye to her family

and leaves for the castle.

Asha and Valentino visit

their friends in the castle's kitchen.

The seven teens work together.

Asha tells them she is nervous

to meet with King Magnifico.

She wants to be his helper.

Her pals tell Asha not to worry.
They say that Magnifico grants
the wishes of his helpers
and their families.
Soon, Queen Amaya comes
to bring Asha to the king.

The king protects people's wishes
by hiding them in a special room.
Very few have seen the wishes.
Asha sees Sabino's wish!
His wish is to make something
that will inspire others.

Asha thinks that the wish is beautiful
and asks the king if he would
grant Sabino's wish that night.
But the king fears that the wish
might be dangerous.

Asha promises King Magnifico
that Sabino would never harm others.
But the king is unsure.
He insists he must protect Rosas.
He will only grant wishes that he
feels are best for the kingdom.

At the wish ceremony, the king
does not grant Sabino's wish.
Asha and her family are upset.
Queen Amaya is surprised
when the king tells Asha
that she cannot be his helper.

Asha thinks the king is wrong to
keep people's wishes locked away.
She climbs the wishing tree
and looks at the sky with Valentino.
They see a star sparkling.

Asha believes that everyone
deserves the chance to make
their wish come true.
She wishes on the twinkling star
for a way to help that happen.

The wishing star zooms to Earth
and lights up the land!
It sprinkles stardust on the plants
and animals in the forest,
giving them the power to speak.
Asha is amazed!

The animals say that all living
things are made of stardust.
Asha tells Star that the king has
locked up her family's wishes.
Star will help Asha
rescue the wishes.

Asha, Valentino, and Star sneak
into the king's special room.
They find Sabino's wish!
But before they can look for
Sakina's wish, the king returns.
The three friends hide.

They learn that the king
had noticed Star's light.
He is afraid of anything
more powerful than himself.
He will use a book of evil magic
to try to destroy Star's light.

Asha gives Sabino his wish.
Suddenly, Magnifico arrives
with Sakina's wish.
The king is furious and crushes
Sakina's wish to punish Asha
for stealing from him.

The family escapes with Star.

They hide on a small island.

Asha, Star, and Valentino

will return to Rosas,

determined to rescue all the wishes.

Asha and Star send a mouse
to ask for the queen's help.
Queen Amaya worries that
King Magnifico no longer wants
what is best for the people of Rosas.

The queen agrees to help Asha and
her friends set the wishes free.
Asha makes a plan to distract
King Magnifico and rescue
the wishes of everyone in Rosas.

King Magnifico uses evil magic
to create a powerful staff.
The king plans to capture Star's energy
for himself so he can have
total control of Rosas.
Asha's friends open the castle roof.
Star tries to lead the wishes
from the king's room to the people.

But King Magnifico appears!
He captures Star with his staff
and takes control of the wishes.

The king soon captures Asha, too!
He waves his staff and creates
a giant black cloud in the sky.
The cloud blocks the stars
and covers the kingdom in darkness.

The king tells the people of Rosas
that there will be no more
stars to wish on
and no more hopes and dreams.
He wants to be all-powerful.

Asha remembers that we are all
made of stardust.
She urges the people of Rosas
to join her in challenging the king.
Soon, their voices join hers!

All over Rosas, people's hearts
glow and light up the kingdom.
The light hits King Magnifico,
and his staff starts to shake.
Asha's idea is working!

Star sends out a beam of light
and escapes from the staff.
The king's evil magic is broken!
The cloud disappears,
and the stars shine bright.
Sakina and Sabino return.

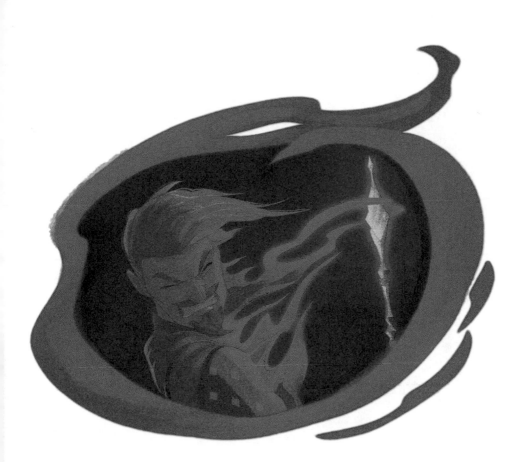

King Magnifico is pulled into

his staff and trapped there forever.

Queen Amaya now leads Rosas!

The wishes float down

and return to the people of Rosas.

Everyone is happy to get them back.

It is time for Star to leave.

Asha worries that she and Rosas

still need Star's help.

But Asha's friends tell her

that she gave them hope

when they needed it most.

Asha feels encouraged.

Star decides to leave behind

a magic wand for Asha.

Star knows that Asha will use

the gift to keep helping others.

Everyone says goodbye to Star.
Sabino and Sakina are happy to
live out their dreams at last.
Asha will never forget
that magic lives in all of us,
because we are all made from stars.